D1282741

THE ALPHABET BOAT

A Seagoing Alphabet Book

by GEORGE MENDOZA

Pictures by LAWRENCE DI FIORI

AMERICAN HERITAGE PRESS
NEW YORK

Book Design: Elaine Gongora

Text Copyright © 1972 by George Mendoza.
Illustrations Copyright © 1972 by Lawrence Di Fiori.
Published by American Heritage Press, a subsidiary of McGraw-Hill, Inc.
Published in Canada by McGraw-Hill Company of Canada, Ltd.

Library of Congress Catalog Card Number: 78-155882
07-041424-6 (trade)
07-041425- 4 (library)

For Nancy Woodward...at last!
And with special thanks to Kathleen Daly

Aa

The boat needs an anchor
to keep us at rest.

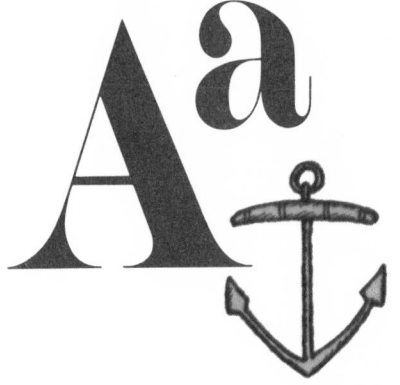

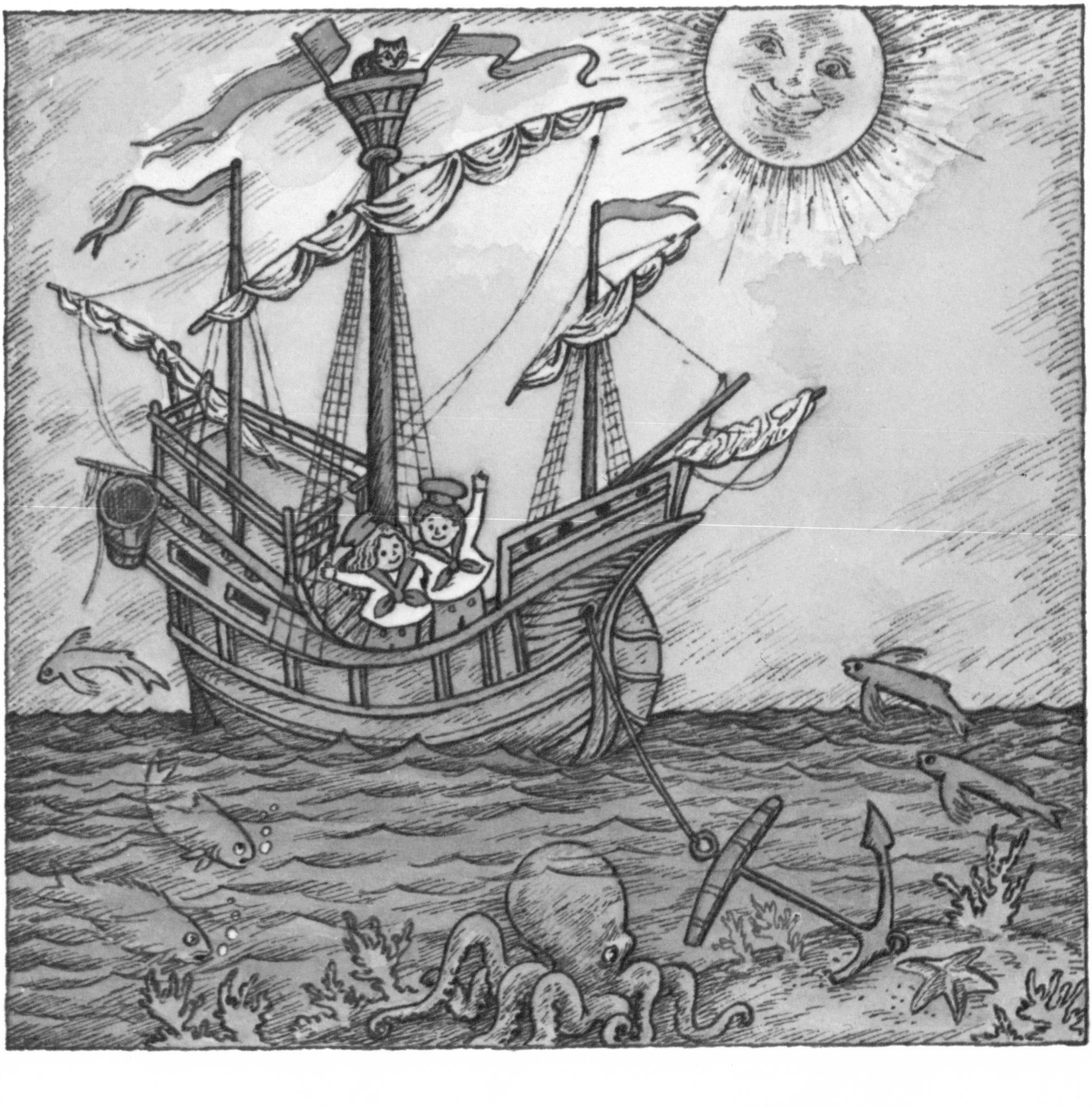

B b

The boat needs a bird
to perch on the bow.

The boat needs a captain
to put us to sea.

Cc

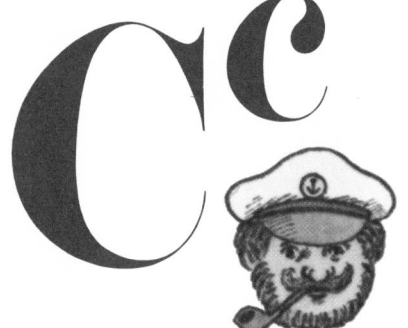

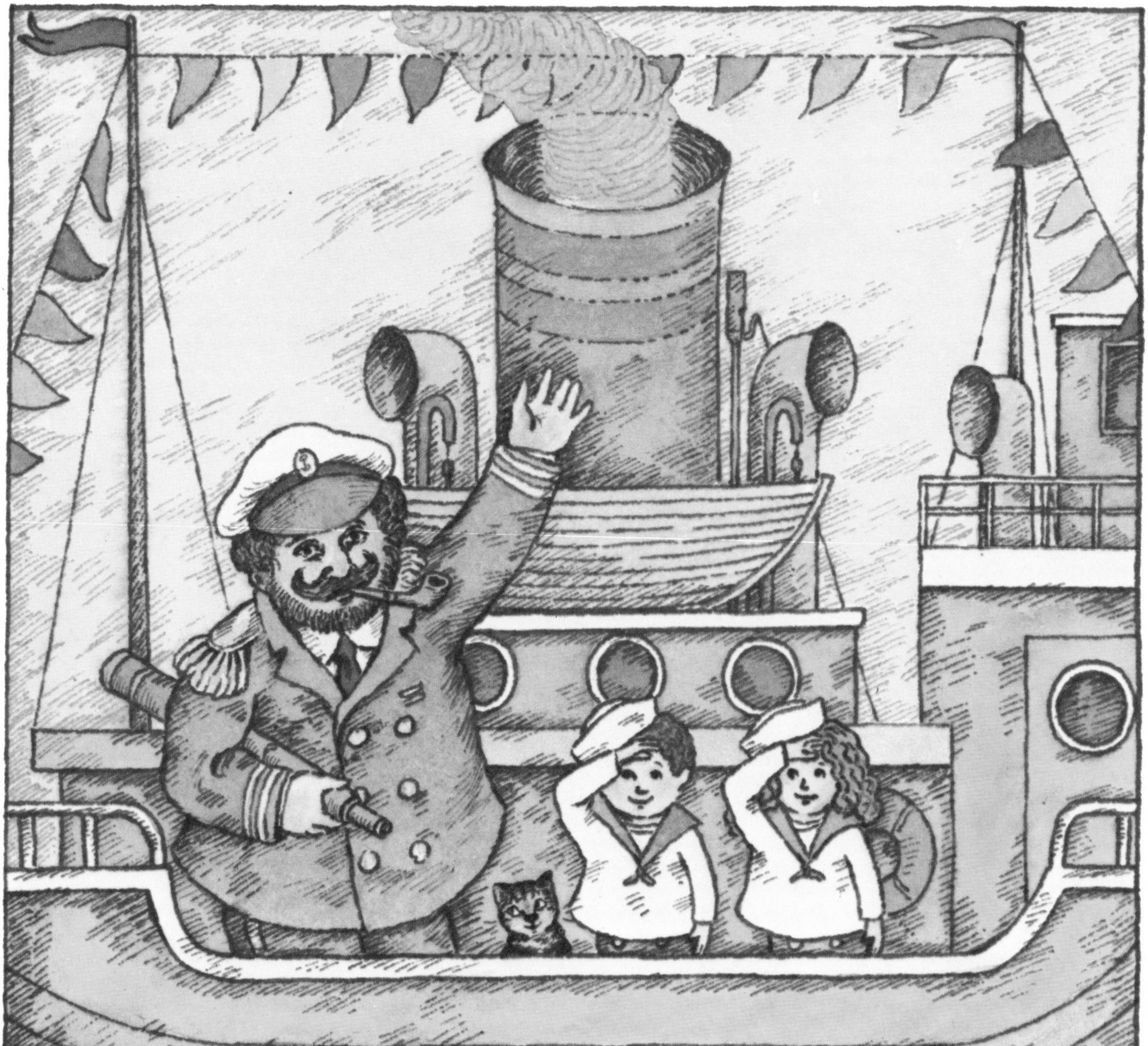

Dd

The boat needs a dinghy
to follow in tow.

Ee

The boat needs an east wind
to fill up the sails.

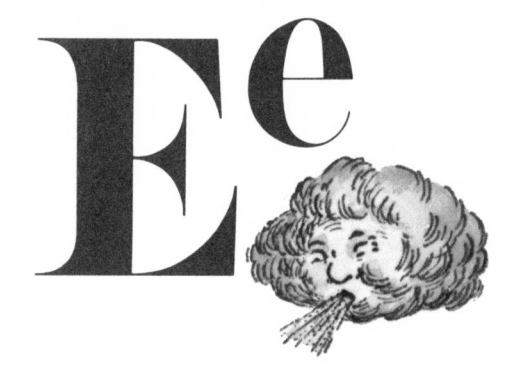

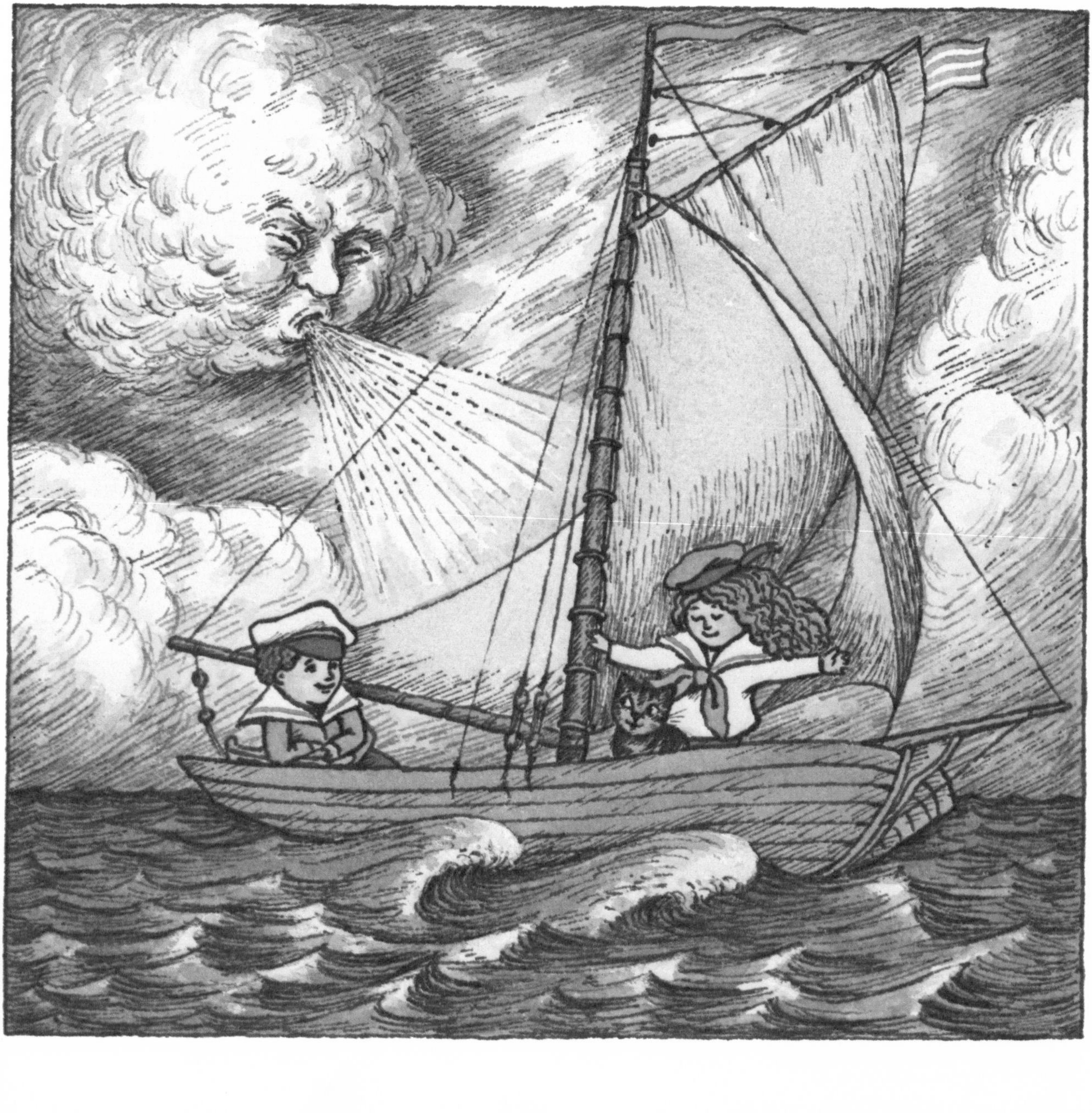

The boat needs a fair sky
for the long journey ahead.

F f

Gg

The boat needs a galley
to store biscuits and rum.

The boat needs a horn
to call through the fog.

H h

Ii

The boat needs an iron keel
to ride out a storm.

Jj

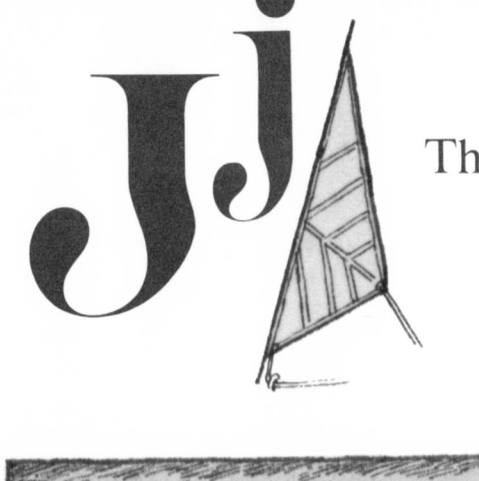

The boat needs a jib sail;
hoist the halyards high!

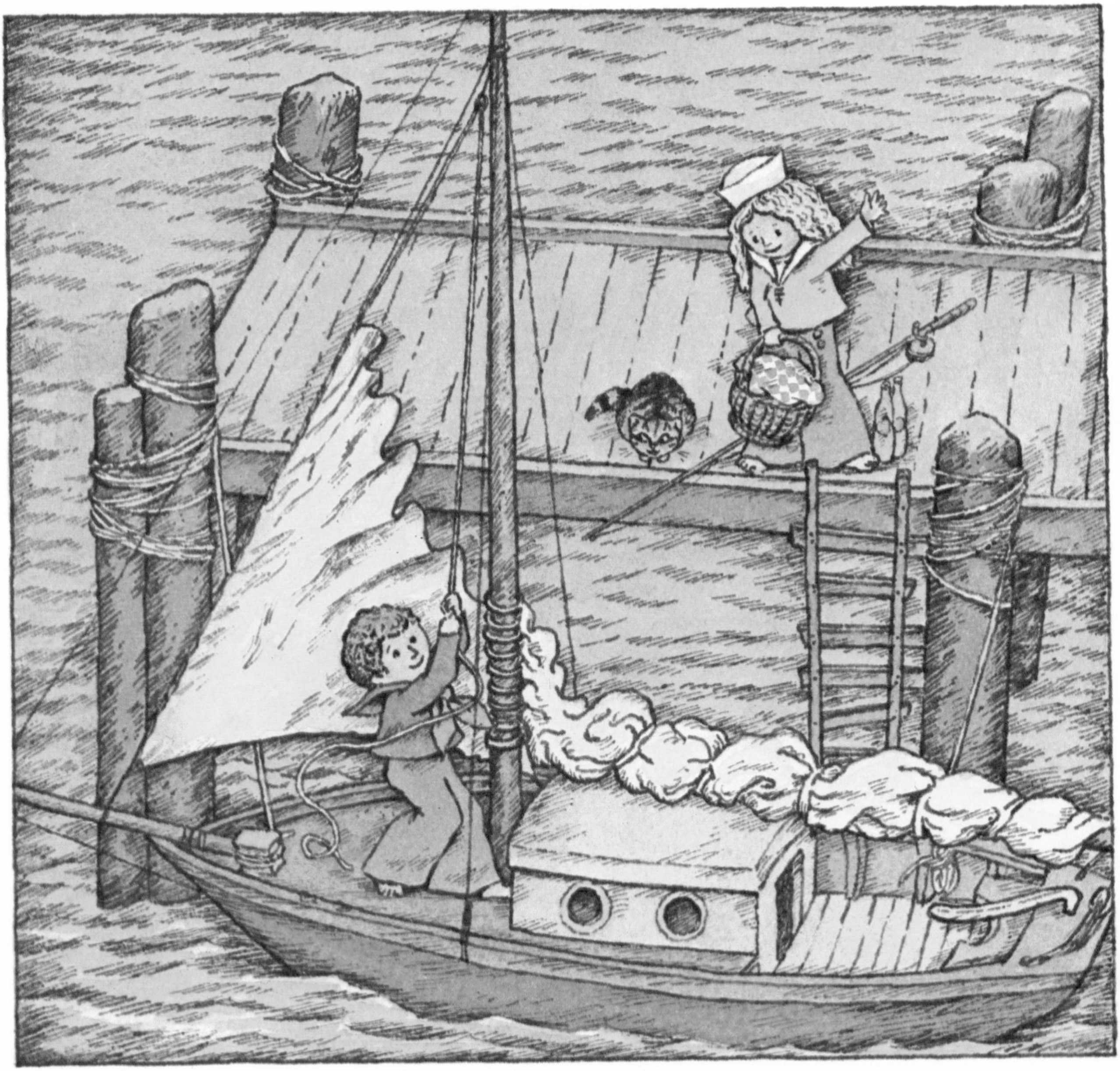

The boat needs a kettle
to brew coffee for the watch.

K k

The boat needs a long glass
for spotting a whale.

L l

Mm

The boat needs a mainsail
for speed in the gathering breeze.

The boat needs a northern light
to wink in the night.

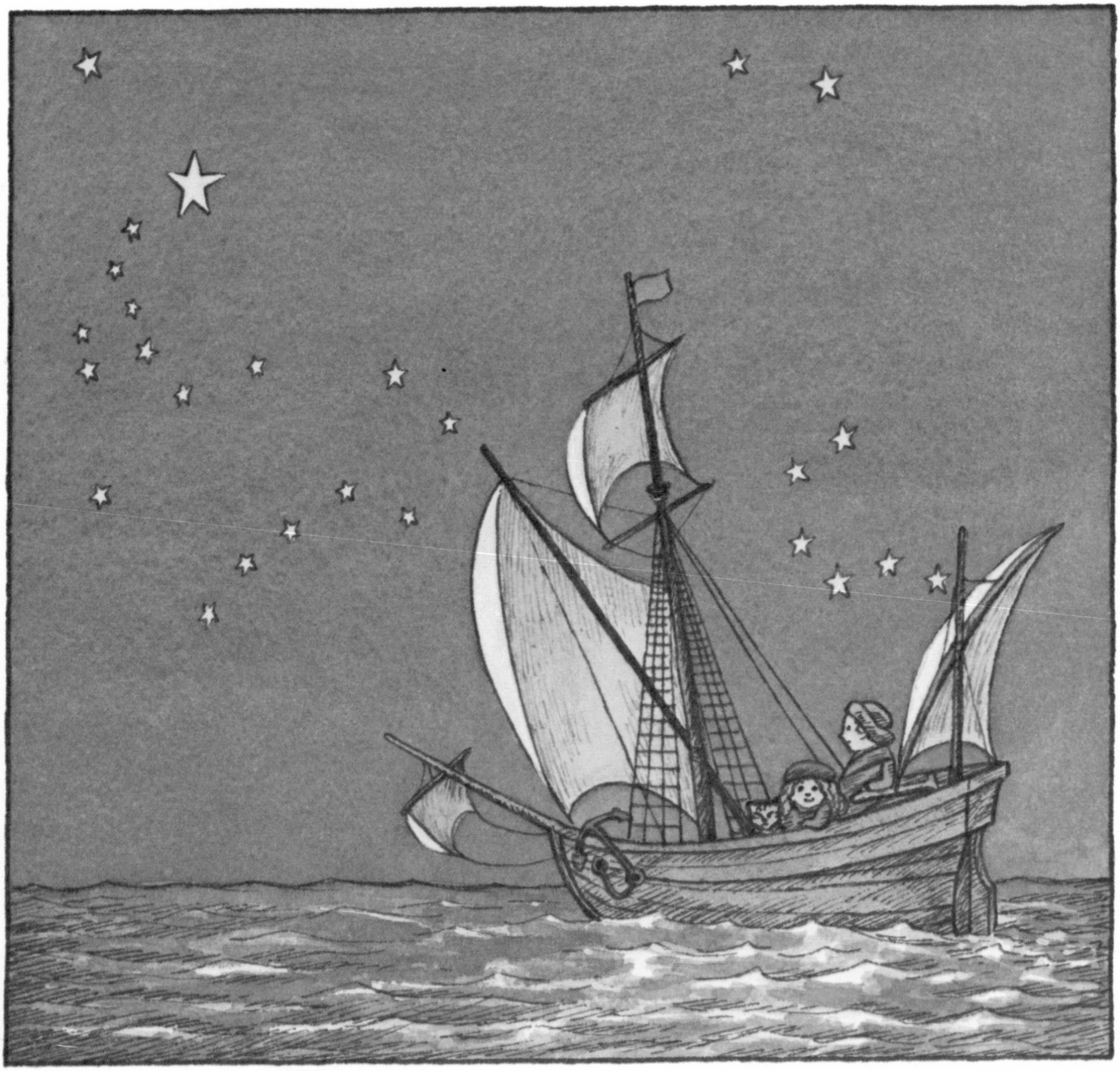

O o

The boat needs oars:
"Drive her, mates, drive her!"

Pp

The boat needs planks,
sturdy pine and white oak.

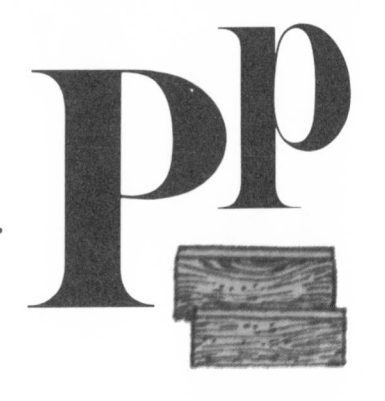

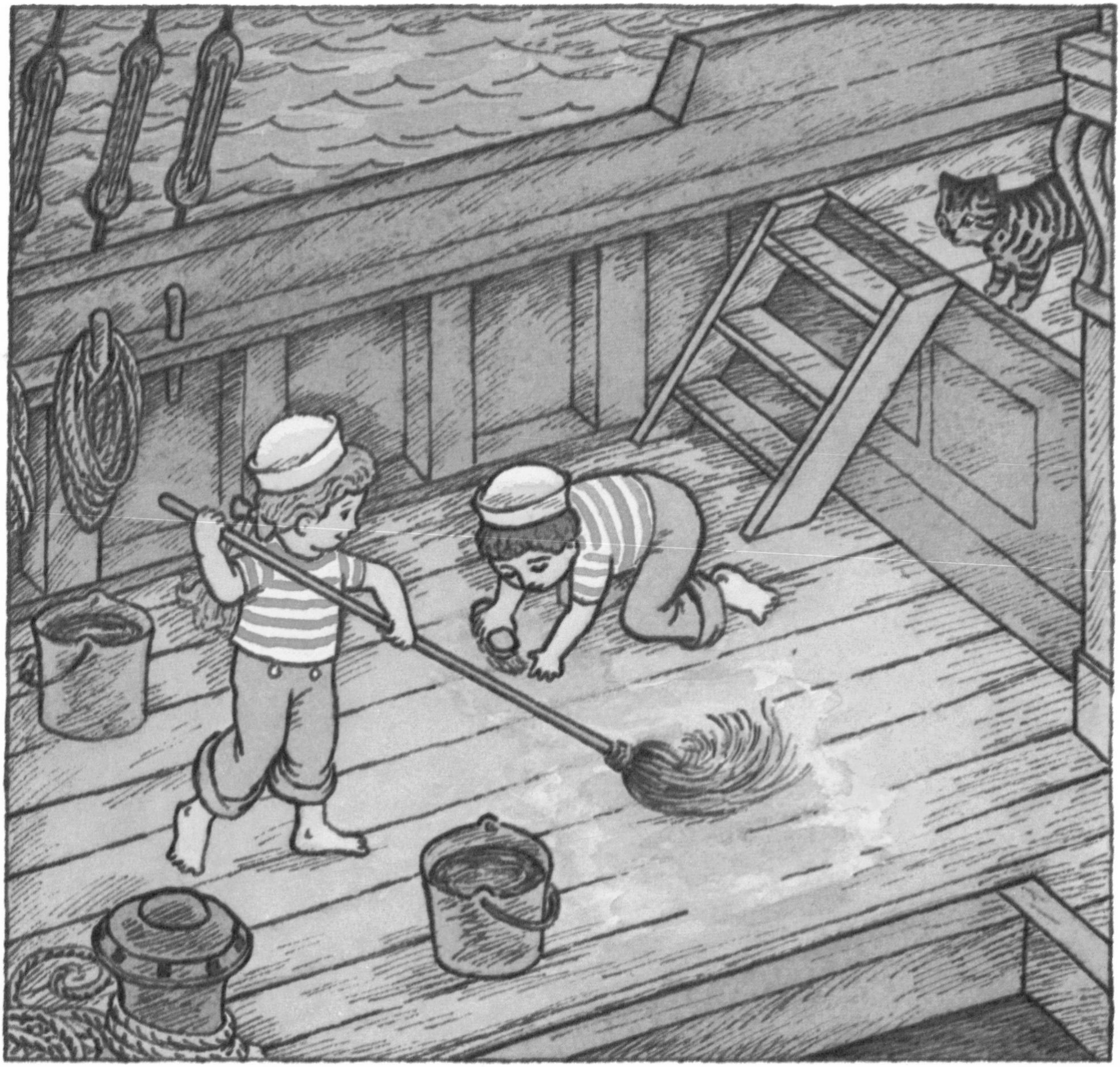

Qq

The boat needs a quiet harbor,
far from the swells and spray.

R r

The boat needs a rudder
to steer through the seas.

Ss

The boat needs a song
to sing under the stars.

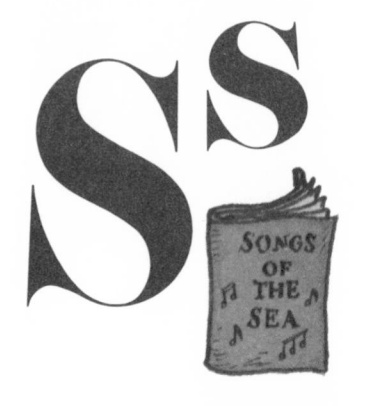

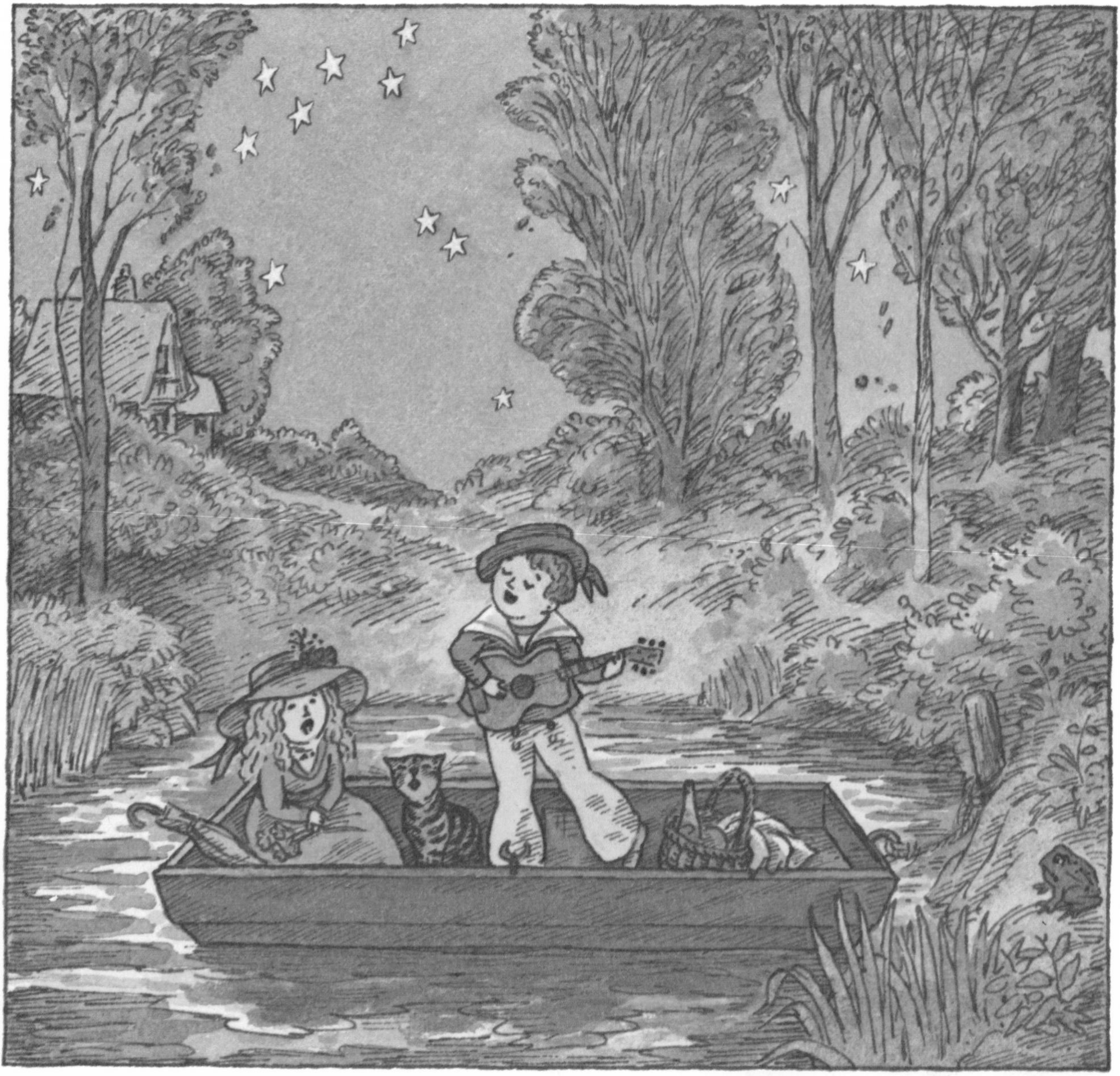

Tt

The boat needs a transom
to carry her name.

Uu

The boat is called umiak
if you are an Eskimo.

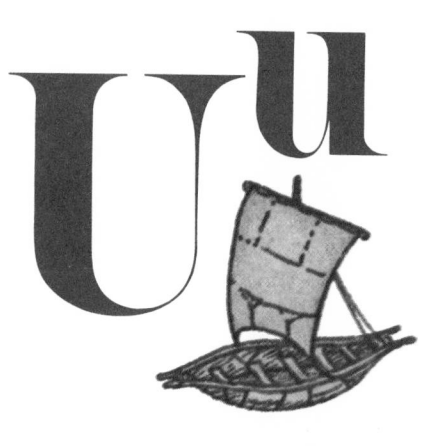

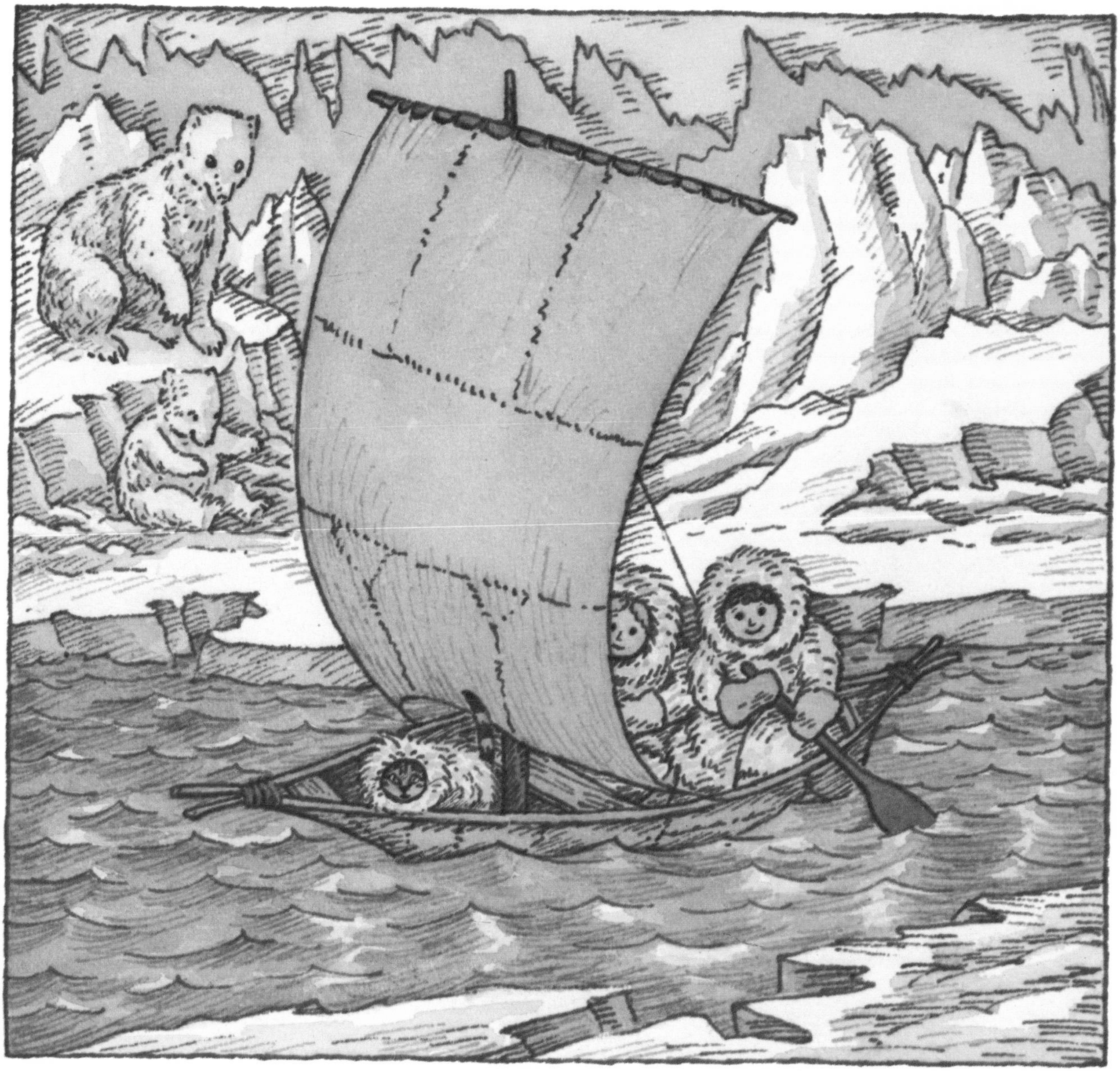

Vv

The boat needs varnish
for her branches of spars.

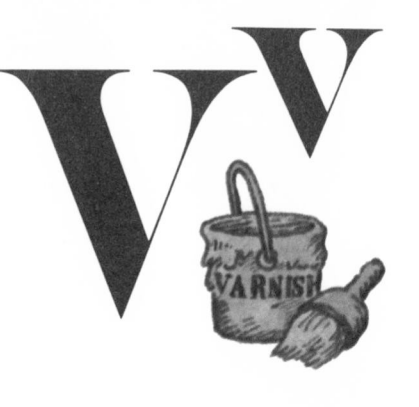

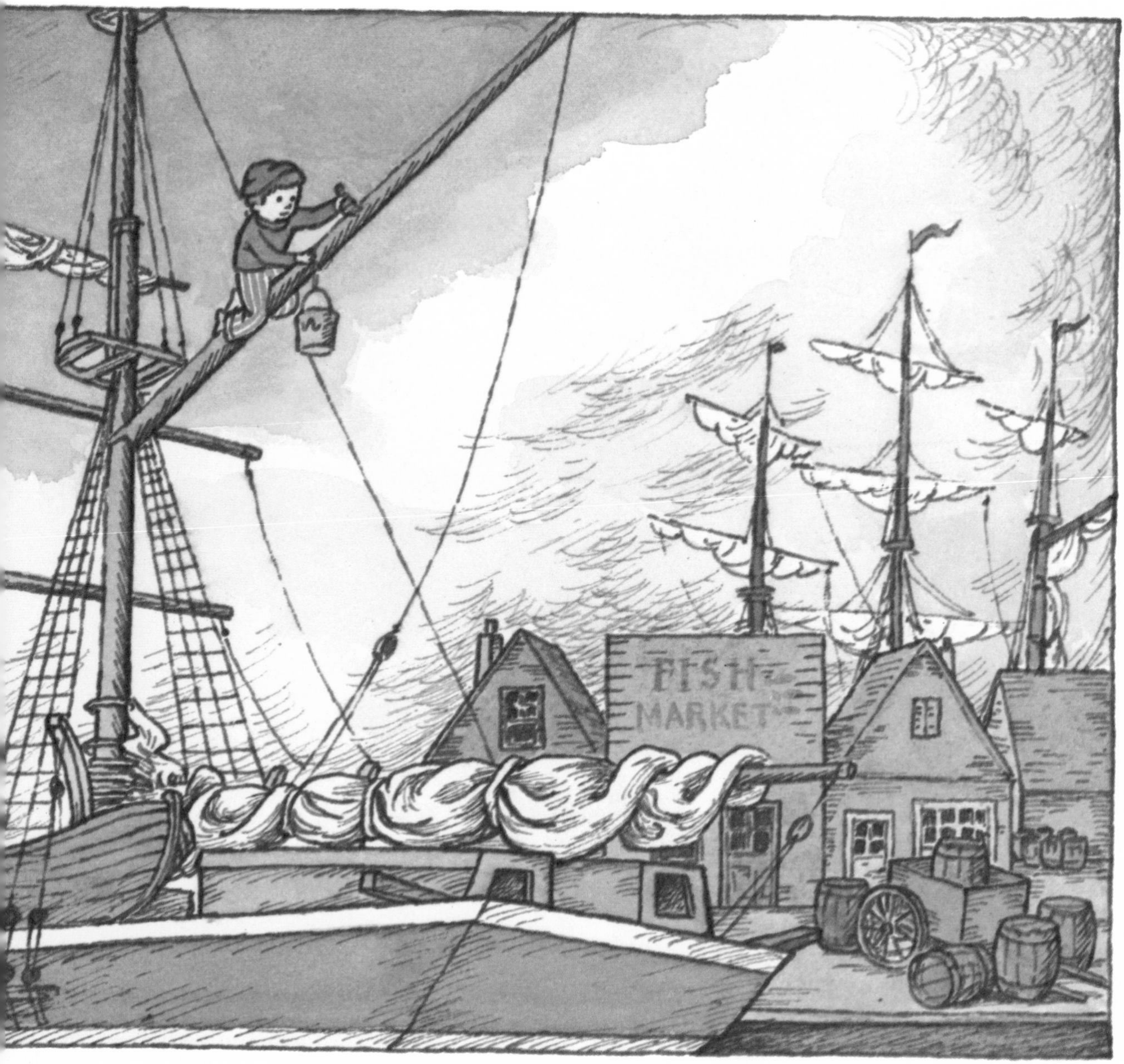

W w

The boat needs a wheel
to hold against tumbling waves.

X x

The boat needs an X
when it is a xebec.

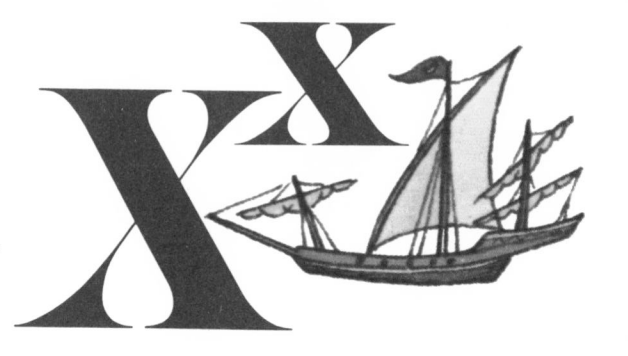

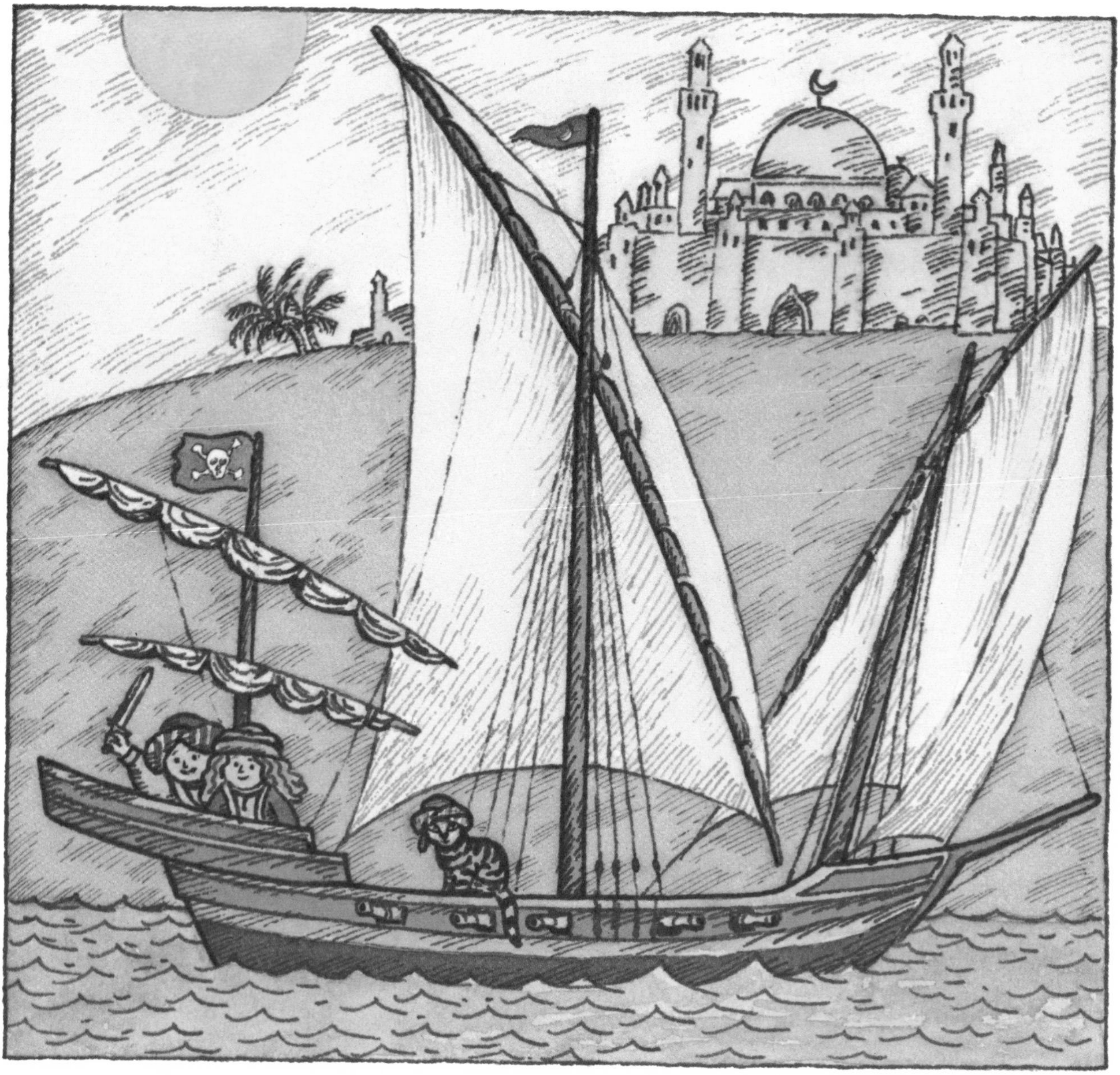

Yy

The boat needs a yellow moon
to pillow your dream.

Z z

The boat needs a zephyr,
  west winds home,
    gentle at your back.